RANGER

THE ESCAPE ARTIST

RADA JONES

APOLODOR

APOLODOR PUBLISHING

1

I'm in luck. These two smell like suckers.

I crawl behind the bushes, waiting for them to lock their car and head down the path to the stand in the forest. I've been here since dawn, hoping that someone shows up. Hunters always bring food, and they're too busy looking for deer to notice me.

They shuffle down the path, and I follow. The woods all around are alive but silent, and a full moon lights the oaks, throwing twisted shadows over the leaf-covered trail. I watch my every step, darting from one shady spot to another, my steps soft as they can be. But a whiff of grilled meat hits my nose and gets me drooling so hard that my tongue hurts and my belly growls. I drop to the ground, worried the humans heard me, but they're too busy talking to give a hoot about what goes on behind them. They only care about their hunt tonight, so I'm safe.

The old one coughs a thick, heavy cough, and spits to the side.

"We'd better be careful. Bill said there's a bear around here. Last week, it raided his food when he left the blind to dress his deer. Watch your back, he said. You don't want to meet one of them monsters."

The tall one shrugs.

"That's BS, just like everything else Bill says. There are no bears here. And if there were, they'd be looking for nuts, roots, and berries. They're not hungry enough to bother people. Not yet. Now, if it was February..."

The old man shrugs and pulls his splotched jacket closer, then shines his flashlight to check behind the trees.

"I dunno, John. He'd barely had three beers when he told me. He even showed me the cooler, all trashed. Looked like a bear to me."

I fall behind a little and keep to the shade to make sure they don't see me. Truth be told, I shouldn't keep that close. I can track them all the way to the blind by smell alone, but I'm so hungry I can't think straight. Last night, I ate nothing but a couple of chicken bones from the KFC parking lot. And nothing at all the night before that. But hungry or not, I'd better be careful around humans and their guns.

Last summer, some humans built a square blind on top of a platform to give them shelter when they hunt. They covered it with dead branches and leaves, and they did a good job.

Between that and the darkness, you'd have a hard time finding it if not for the smell. The place always smells like stress sweat, cigarettes, and beer. And burgers.

Licking my chops, I hide behind a fallen tree to watch the tall, skinny man limp up the steps. His pant leg rides up, and his left ankle shines in the moonlight. It smells like metal. The old man follows, wheezing and coughing on every step. They drop their packs in the blind, then walk back out to check the mud for hoof tracks and the trees for scars.

"This here's a good one."

Wheezy shines his flashlight on a slender ash tree leaning over the crossing of the paths, and Skinny spreads some doe scent over the scarred tree and the bushes around it. They return to their stand just as a gust of wind fills my nose with the stench of fake doe piss. It's so strong it chokes me, but that doesn't bother them as they ready their guns and settle to wait.

I squeeze under the dwarf cedar behind them. Here, I'm out of the wind and safe. They couldn't see me in bright daylight, let alone on a cloudy night.

They chat softly and sip on their beers. I don't know what they're saying, and I don't care. All I care about is the cooler.

I wait and wait until Wheezy comes out to pee, all panting and hacking. I wonder why he's here, freezing his butt in the woods when he has food to eat and a warm place to sleep in. How can these humans think the deer won't notice them, as stupid as deer are? These two talk, cough, and fart so much that I could hear them from the road. And they stink. The smell of their beer and their piss carries for miles, even though they sprayed themselves with something that smells like the cedars after the snowfall. But that's still far away. Leaves have only started changing, but these two already smell like rotten leaves and snow.

Mom was right. You can't understand humans. You shouldn't trust them, either. Trust no one but yourself, she taught me, and that served me right my whole life.

Something darts behind the trees. It's a small doe, and she's fast. The humans go quiet, and the feral scent of their sweat fills my nose. I wait for them to shoot, but they don't. I wonder why, when I see a big buck chasing the doe, and a shot blasts the night's silence.

The buck leaps over a dead tree like a bird. He's about to vanish when a second shot finds him and stops him in mid-flight. He crashes to the ground, screaming, and rolls in a cloud of scattered leaves. The coppery scent of his blood fills my nostrils as life pours out of him, and my stomach flips.

I don't enjoy killing. Sure, I'll chase a rat or a squirrel when I've got nothing else, but that gives me no joy. Unlike humans, who grin as they take pictures of themselves with their kill. Where's the fun in that?

Oh, well. The buck is dead. My time has come. I'll sneak in and grab the food while they fool with the deer.

I force myself to wait until they're halfway down the path, going to check their kill, then I squeeze inside the blind. The food is in a big plastic cooler, and the smell makes me slobber like crazy, but the darn box is zipped closed, and I can't open it. I bite it and claw at it, trying to rip it apart, but it's made of tough stuff and my claws barely leave a mark. Darn. I'm running out of time. I'll just take it all.

I grab it and run, but the thing is big and heavy. It dangles between my front paws, so I can't even walk with it, let alone run. Dang it. In utter despair, I turn sideways and drag it on the ground.

The box drops from one step to the next, making enough noise to wake the dead. But there's nothing I can do but try to rush. I do my best to hustle, but I stumble upon it and roll down the steps in a terrible ruckus.

The men hear me and shout something. I don't know what they say, but I know I should drop the cooler and run. But I can't. I'm too hungry. And, as slow as I am dragging this monster down the trail, they're even slower, with their wheezing and coughing and metal legs. I keep at it. Two more steps and I can hide behind the bushes.

A shot rings out.

Something slashes my cheek, then my chest explodes. I drop the cooler and crash to the ground, rolling in a cloud of fallen leaves, just like the deer.

They shot me.

My heart pumps like I'm running, but I'm not. I'm lying on the ground, struggling to catch my breath as air whooshes out of me in salty bubbles. I'm panting, but I still can't get enough air. I try to crawl, but I have no strength left.

The humans shuffle closer.

"What the heck is this?" Wheezy asks, and Skinny shines a flashlight in my eyes.

"It's a dog. It's a goddamn dog. What on earth is a dog doing here?"

"You're right. It looks like a Golden Retriever. He's bleeding out."

"Darn it. Just what we needed," Skinny says. "Like we didn't have enough work with that deer."

Wheezy sighs and shakes his head.

"Son of a gun. Let's take him to the vet."

He tries to lift me, but can't. He swears and turns to Skinny.

"Come help me get him in the car."

Skinny shrugs.

"There's no point. It's almost midnight, so they're all closed. And we still have to deal with that deer. We'll take him in the morning if he makes it through the night."

Wheezy shakes his head.

"I can't. I just can't let him die. Why don't you stay and dress the deer while I take the dog to the emergency vet down the road? I'll come back to get you after. Just help me get him in the car."

They lean over me, and I flash my teeth and growl. I don't

want any human touching me, and I'm not going anywhere. I'll die right here, where I lived.

But I'm too weak to breathe, let alone put up a fight. All I can do is gurgle as they roll me onto someone's jacket to drag me to their car. Oh, how I wish I could run, but I can't even breathe. My life drains away with my blood.

2

———————

I'm so weak I have no fight left in me as they push me into that stinky car. The stench of old cigarette smoke and gasoline hits me so bad it would take my breath away if I had any left.

Skinny slams the door behind me as Wheezy gets in the driver's seat and starts the engine. The car roars and takes off, spitting gravel and sliding through the mud. My chest bursts into flames each time we drop from one pothole to another; Wheezy coughs and curses, but he doesn't slow down. And he talks. And talks.

"How ya doing, boy? Just a few minutes, and we'll get to the paved road. That's gonna be easier. Then another half an hour or so, and we'll be at the emergency vet at Exit 40. They're open 24/7, and they're good. They took care of my Buddy when he was sick. But that was long ago. Poor Buddy crossed the rainbow bridge last winter."

I don't know what he's blabbering, nor do I care. I'm way too busy struggling to breathe.

"What's your name, boy? And what were you doing in the woods? A handsome boy like you has got to have a home. Though come to think of it, you don't have a collar. Are you lost? Did you run away?"

I stop listening to work on my breathing. It shouldn't be hard. Air in, air out. Repeat. Something gets stuck in my throat and chokes me, and I hack out a blob of blood. I sniff it. It smells like blood. I lay my nose on my paws and close my eyes. I don't feel good. I'm so weak and shaky that I forget I'm supposed to be scared. This is my first time in a car since some humans trapped me and locked me in their van, long ago. They took me to the shelter, but I squeezed between their legs and took off when they opened the door. But I won't be that lucky this time. I can't even breathe, let alone run.

Wheezy keeps at it.

"Sorry I shot you, boy. I thought you were the bear Bill told us about, and I wanted to scare you away. I didn't know you were a dog. But I bet you that the vet will fix you. I took a bullet in the chest in Iraq too, you know. I thought I was dying, but then they shoved a tube inside my chest. To expand the lung, they said, whatever that means. A week later, I was as good as new. Well, a few weeks maybe. They let me go home. I'll bet you'll get better in no time, OK?"

He keeps talking, but my heart is racing and pounding so loud it drowns out his words. Then my eyes gray out, and my brain fogs like I'm sinking into a dark pit. I wonder if that's how Mom felt when the truck hit her.

3

Where the heck am I?

I'm not dead, I don't think, since I'm still breathing. But everything hurts. My whole chest is on fire, and so is my left cheek. But nothing's half as bad as the smell. Whatever this place is, it stinks of pain and fear. And some awful chemicals that smell even worse.

I open my eyes. The right one, that is, since the left one is covered. I paw at it, but it hurts, so I stop.

I try to check where I'm at, but I can only see straight ahead. It's like there's something around my head that blocks my side vision. I shake my head to ditch it, but the searing pain in my chest makes me stop. Drat.

I turn my head gently to see that I'm inside a metal cage, lying on a rug that stinks of bleach. And I'm not alone. All around, there's a hundred cells just like mine, and they're all full of dogs.

I've never seen so many dogs together. Big dogs, small dogs, yappy dogs, quiet dogs, of every color and gender and breed. Some snore with their noses under their tails, some sniff the breeze, others clean their privates or bark nonsense at each other. The black pup to my left is crying for his mom, but no one answers. He keeps yelling until he grows hoarse, then falls asleep with his nose on his paws. The white bulldog to my right is missing an eye and half of an ear, but he's keeping his good eye glued to the beagle on his other side. I can't imagine why. I can smell from right here that she's spayed.

Right across from my cell, an orange Golden Retriever sniffs my way. He wags his tail to say hi like he knows me, but I don't think we ever met.

"What's up, Bro? How are you doing?" he barks.

I cock my head.

"Me?"

"Yep. What's your name?"

"My name?"

"Sure, Bro. I'm Prozak. Sergeant Prozak. You?"

"I... I'm not sure. Dog, I guess?"

"Of course. We're all dogs here. That's what humans call us. But what's the name that sets you apart from other dogs? What do your friends call you?"

"I... I don't have many friends."

"You don't have many friends? How come? A Golden like you?"

All of a sudden, I feel guilty. Like I stole a pup's bone, or something.

"I'm a bit of a drifter. I keep moving from one place to another and don't stay put for too long."

The white bulldog next to me takes his good eye off the beagle.

"So, you're one of those, eh? A stray."

Prozak's hackles go up. He curls his lip and flashes his canines at the bulldog.

"That's rude, you know. That is no way to speak to a fellow just because he's a bit down on his luck."

The bulldog tucks his tail and flattens his half-ear.

"Sorry, Sarge. I didn't mean it that way. But if he doesn't even have a name…"

"Sure he does. His name's Ranger," Prozak says.

"How do you know? And what does that mean?" I ask.

"I know it because I just made it up. And it means that you're one of those folks who likes to go places and check on things."

I wag my tail.

"That's me, all right, always going places and checking on things. I like it. Thanks."

"Anytime. Tell me, what happened to you?"

"I... I got shot."

"Really? How?"

"I followed some hunters, and I got too close. How about you?"

Prozak flattens his ears.

"I was careless."

"What did you do?"

"I work for the Border Patrol, and I sniffed some stuff I shouldn't have. And I should have known better. My job is to find contraband — drugs, money, hidden humans. But those who smuggle them don't want them found, so they tricked me into sniffing some poison. I barely made it out alive. But I'm better now. They say I'll be out in a few days."

I cock my head right, then left, then right again, to understand what he's saying, but I can't. I'd think he's lying if I couldn't smell that he's honest. He's a decent pup, and a Golden, like me. Though he looks real, while I'm... who knows what I am?

"What's work?"

Prozak cocks his head left to stare at me.

"What?"

Oops.

"What is it like to work for the Border Patrol?"

"Not bad. I get to sniff every car, truck, and all the people who cross the border to make sure they have nothing they shouldn't. If they're clean, I let them go. If I sniff something funky, I sit to point it to my handler, and he gives me a treat."

"You have a handler? What's a handler?"

"That's my human. He feeds me and takes me out for walks. I find stuff for him and look after him."

"Wow."

"You don't have a human?"

I shake my head no, but my cheek feels like it'll split open, so I stop.

Prozak's ears drop in distress.

"Wow! I'm so sorry! That's terrible! So, who feeds you? Who takes you out for walks? And, more importantly, who do you look after?"

I yawn. This is getting awkward.

"I find my own food. That often has me walking more than I'd like. And I do my best to look after myself."

"But who scratches your ears? And who gives you baths?" Prozak asks.

"I scratch my ears with my hind paws. And I take mud baths whenever it rains."

"But who tells you that you are a good boy? And who's your responsibility? What's your mission?" Prozak growls.

His ears have dropped so low they stuck to his head. He's so concerned I'd rather not tell him what humans say to me when they see me. It's either "filthy mongrel" or "dirty thief," unless it's "mangy mutt." But Prozak doesn't need to know that.

"I don't have any responsibilities. I just live, you know. I go places. I sniff things. I stay alive."

Prozak's tail tucks between his legs to touch his chin. He's horrified.

"But that's just terrible! You're missing the very best thing in life: having someone to love."

I cock my head, wondering if he's serious. Yep. He is. I can smell it. Poor dog. Nice guy, Prozak, but he got brainwashed by the humans. Maybe it's not his fault, but the truth is the truth.

I wag my tail to soften the blow.

"I beg to differ. The best thing in life is freedom. There's nothing better than being your own master, going where you want and doing what you want when it suits you. Nothing beats that."

Prozak sighs.

"I don't think so, Ranger. There's nothing better than being with someone you love, looking after them, giving them joy, and having them love you back. Nothing. Not the food, not the walks, not even the praise. Love is the best thing there is."

4

─────────

Prozak is nuts. But I don't want to be rude, so I wag my tail left to tell him to cut it out, and he does. Then we chat. He tells me about his job and his human, and I tell him about life on the street.

"Have you always been a free dog?" he asks.

"Almost. My mom had seven of us in a shed, behind a woodpile. She did her best to care for us, but the streets were cold, and the food was scarce, so only two of us made it. Then Mom got hit by a truck, and we were left all alone. We were just pups, still getting used to being on our own, when we got dognapped by two men in a van. They tricked us with hot dogs, caught us in a net, then locked us in a van. When the door opened, I managed to squeeze between their legs and escaped, but my sister didn't, and I never saw her again. I don't know what happened to her. That was two winters ago. Since then, I've been on my own."

Prozak cocks his head.

"Doesn't it get lonely at times?"

I lick my paw to think better.

"I guess. Nights are harsh, especially in winter. They feel like they'll last forever when there's nobody to curl against to keep you warm. An empty belly makes you feel even colder. Once in a while, when I feel like the night will never end, I wonder what's the point. Why not just let myself fall asleep in the snow and never wake up? But then the sun comes up and I catch a whiff of bacon, or some kid drops a cookie, and all is well with the world."

"Until sunset."

"Yeah, until sunset. How did you know?"

Prozak sighs.

"It's the same with me. Nights are always harsh. Days keep you busy with this and that — places to go, people to sniff — but at night, you're all alone with your dreams. I always dream of my first humans, Father and Ruby. When I wake up, I feel even lonelier."

"What happened to them?"

Prozak's ears flatten, and I catch the bitter smell of his sorrow.

"I'm not sure. But that was long ago. Tell me about you. Where will you go when you get better?"

"Back to the streets, I guess. Though winter's coming, and every winter gets harder as you age."

"Tell me about it," Prozak says.

But I didn't get to. They took him away the day after that, and I never saw him again. I still think about him now and then. I wonder if he ever found his humans. I hope he did.

But most of the time, I'm too busy to think. These humans are a full-time job.

Every day, they wrap my muzzle in something so I can't bite, then they take me to the man they call the vet. He pokes and prods me while others stick me with needles and rip off my bandages. They even washed me, for Dog's sake, in some filthy water with no mud, just some stinky chemicals that itched like crazy.

"It's all good, Ranger. You'll feel so much better when you get rid of the mange and the fleas," the vet said.

But I didn't. Feel better, that is. Having their hands all over me when they washed me was bad enough, but when they grabbed my paws to clip my nails, I went berserk. I couldn't even lick myself clean afterwards because of the cone around my neck. A harrowing experience. I wouldn't recommend it unless you're into horror. The only decent part is the food. Crunchy and plentiful, and I don't even have to steal it.

But I'm getting better, despite their care. I'm breathing easier, and my chest stopped hurting. They even took off the eye patch and the cone, so I can scratch properly. But for the collar, of course. They put that miserable thing around my neck, and I can't ditch it. Dog knows I tried. I scratched myself bloody and twisted myself into a pretzel to bite it off, but I couldn't. So I'm learning to live with it.

The vet seems pleased.

"You're on the mend, boy. A few more days, and you're ready to go."

"Where will he go?" the girl helping him asks. She's not that bad, that one. She always slips me an extra treat when they're done with torturing me.

"We'll send him to the shelter, Marylin. They'll do their best to socialize him to get him adopted, but it's gonna be tough."

"Why? He's handsome, even with that scar."

"He may be handsome, but he's wild. Seeing how he acts, I don't think he ever lived in a home, and I'm afraid he's too old to learn. See, Marilyn, the things that helped him survive in the streets — his suspicion, cunning, and stealth — will make it hard for him to thrive in a home. A nice pet must be trusting, loyal, and loving. He's none of those things. Just look at how he glares at us."

Marilyn shrugs.

"Of course he does, because we hurt him every time we touch him. If someone treats him with kindness and patience, he'll respond in kind."

The vet shrugs.

"I hope you're right, Marilyn, but I don't think so. I think he's too old to change."

5

The day they coaxed me into a crate that they then loaded into a van, I knew it was time. It was now or never if I was to escape. Ever since they locked me in that cage, I chewed on the darn bars until I got my muzzle bleeding, but I didn't make a dent. If they took me to another place like this, it was over. I needed to flee on the way.

I waited until the van door slammed shut, then tried to chew on the lock, but the space between the bars was too small for my muzzle; I tried to slide the thing open with my paw, like I saw the humans do it, but I couldn't. I needed one of those damn opposable thumbs.

Oh well. It is what it is. I'll just wait until they open the door and dash out, I told myself. But it was not meant to be.

When the van finally stopped, they rolled my crate into a nasty building that smelled like dogs, cats, and bleach, but they didn't open my door until it faced an open cage. All I could do was to step from the crate into another cell. I was jailed again.

But this one wasn't that bad.

The vet was gone, and so was the daily torture, but the food kept coming. Even some treats. I had three cats to bark at, and the other dogs kept to themselves. Not that bad, other than the schooling.

"You're a good boy, Ranger. Look at you! You're smart and handsome. But if you want to ever find a home, there are a few things you will need to learn," Ella said.

She was the Alpha here, and everyone did as she said. Not the cats, of course — those jerks never do — but the dogs and the humans did their best to please her, so I did too.

She clipped her leash to my collar and taught me to walk her. First inside, then out in the yard, where the wind smelled like gasoline and freedom. The first thing I did was check the fence, of course, but it was way too tall to jump, even if I wasn't tied to a leash with a human at the end. But there was a bit of grass to pee on, even though it smelled like a million other dogs. I stopped to sniff the news, of course, but Ella called me and pulled on her leash. She offered me a treat, so I walked. That's how I taught her to give me treats every time I sat, lay down, and stayed.

The one tricky thing was NO.

It always came at the worst possible moment. Like when I jumped in the mud, lunged at another dog, or barked at cats.

Ella and I squabbled. She persisted, but I was dogged. So, after the umpteenth time she tried to stop me from barking at the tabby cat across the aisle and failed, she gave in and moved it elsewhere.

"I guess you'll have to go to a home without cats," she mumbled. "I hope we can get you to get along with other dogs, at least."

That one was hit or miss. Some dogs just rubbed me the wrong way. I just caught a whiff, and my hackles went up. I had to rip them apart. I didn't know why, but I knew they deserved it. But other dogs I didn't mind sniffing the breeze with. Like my old friend Prozak. Or Charlie, a little curly mutt I made friends with.

All in all, it wasn't bad. I didn't need to dodge cars, rummage through trash and fight other dogs for my dinner. I didn't need to sleep in the snow, chew the ice between my toes or lick my paws to stop them from freezing. I didn't have to be on the lookout for the men in the van. I even had Charlie to hang out with.

But I wasn't free.

I couldn't come and go as I pleased. I couldn't chase squirrels, track hunters, or sniff the wind tickling my nose. I was where the humans wanted me to be, and I only did what they wanted me to do. I missed my freedom, but the other dogs didn't get it. To them, it was all about having a roof above their heads.

"Guess what, Ranger?" Ella said one day.

"What?"

"Someone's here to see you."

I cocked my head left.

"Me?"

Who'd come to see me? Prozak maybe? I'd love to see him again.

But it wasn't Prozak. It was Wheezy.

He limped a little and coughed up a storm, but he had a big smile on his face and smelled like treats.

"How ya doing, boy? Wow, don't you look good, all clean and healed and such? And the scar's not too bad. Makes you look like a pirate."

I didn't know what a pirate was, nor did I care. But the strip of beef jerky he slipped to me smelled good, so I let him pet me.

"How's he doing?" he asked Elle.

"Much better. He's very smart. He already learned to walk, sit, and stay. He's a good boy, but he hates cats."

Wheezy started laughing, then broke into a cough.

"So do I. I'd like to adopt him."

Ella looked him up and down and sighed.

"Are you sure? Ranger's a little frisky, and he's not really socialized yet. To be honest, I'm not sure he'll ever be. He's quite a handful. How about a mellower dog, like little Charlie, here? He needs a home. He's good with other dogs and even cats and…"

"No, thanks. I want my boy, Ranger. I couldn't sleep since that night I shot him. I kept dreaming about him. He reminds me of my Buddy, who died last year. I want to take him home."

"If you're sure…"

"I am."

"OK then. Let's go through the paperwork, then we'll take Ranger for a walk and see how it goes."

6

I watch them leave and lay my nose on my paws, wondering what this is about. Why would Wheezy want to see me? I haven't seen him since the night he shot me, and I didn't even get to taste that burger! What the heck does he want?

In the cell across from mine, Charlie melts into an orange puddle smelling like misery and starts whining as he licks his paws.

"You're going to your forever home. Boy, how I wish it were me."

I crack my left eye open.

"What are you yapping about?"

"Didn't you hear them? That guy came to take you home."

"Wheezy?"

"You know him?"

"Yeah. He shot me. What's a home?"

"It's where you stay inside with the humans. They feed you every day, and play with you, and sometimes they even give you treats. In the morning, they take you for walks to collect your poop in little baggies. But only if there's someone there to see them; otherwise, they leave it there for others to step in."

I cock my head to understand.

"And you like that? To have your poop collected in little baggies?"

Charlie shakes.

"Not the poop part, but I love the food and the treats. And sleeping inside, especially in winter, when it's nice to be warm and dry. And I wouldn't mind having someone to play with. I feel lonely sometimes."

"But you already have all that here, don't you?"

Charlie yawns, and I know he's upset. Dogs only yawn when they're in trouble. When they're tired, they just lie down and sleep.

"I do, but not for long. If nobody wants me, they'll…"

His ears drop, and his tail tucks between his legs to his chin.

"They'll what?"

"They'll put me to sleep to make room for others."

The stench of his fear hits my nose, making my heart feel

hollow and sad. I wish I could help him, but what can I do? Encourage him, I guess.

"No, they won't. I'm sure you'll find a home, if that's what you want. You're a good-looking little fellow, and you're good with dogs and even with cats," I bark.

Charlie shakes his head until his ears slap his face.

"No, I'm not. I hate cats. I'm so scared of them I piss myself."

Wow! What can you say to someone who comes right out and confesses he's afraid of cats? And it's not about the fear. Every dog is afraid of cats, even Rottweilers, because those evil hissy felines are ferocious. No dog can be half as heartless as those sneaky devils. But I would never admit it, for fear that I'd lose everyone's respect.

I scratch my ear to think, but that gets nowhere. So I decide to clean my privates instead. That always gets me into a thoughtful mood.

"Were you born on the streets?" I ask.

Charlie jumps back like I slapped him.

"Of course not! Are you kidding? I grew up in a home full of loving humans. My mom always had a good word and a treat for me, and Dad took me out to play fetch. The kids always slipped me food under the table and I could sleep in any bed I wanted. They even gave me baths!"

"Like, mud baths?"

"Of course not! Real baths, with shampoo and warm water. They even brushed my teeth."

My heckles go up, and I shudder.

"That's horrific! Did you bite them?"

Charlie shakes.

"Of course not! I'd never do something like that!"

"So then, what happened? How did you end up here?"

Charlie smells so sad it breaks my heart.

"One day they started packing. Dad loaded my stuff in the truck and brought me to the shelter. The kids cried when he took me, but he told them they'll come back for me as soon as they found a place to live. 'But why?' I asked. 'This is good enough. I love it here.' Mom cried and hugged me. 'We'll come back to get you, I promise,' she said."

"And?"

"They didn't. I waited and waited, keeping my nose on the door and jumping to my paws whenever it opened, but it was never them."

"I'm sorry," I growl.

"Me too." Charlie curls with his nose under his tail like he's sleeping, but his rancid smell of despair fills the place.

"You know Ranger, for so long I hoped they'd come back to get me, but that hope died long ago. I don't know what happened to them, but I know they won't come back for me. I started hoping that maybe someone else would want me. Somewhere, there must be a human who needs a companion with a loving heart. Someone to scratch my ears and pet me, and tell me about their day. Someone I can watch when they eat, and follow into the bathroom, and welcome home every time they open the door like they've been gone forever, even if they were only out to get the mail. Someone to love who'd love me in return. But there is no one. No one. No wonder. Who'd want to love an old mutt with a cowardly heart?"

His sadness digs a hole in my heart, so deep that my heart feels even more hungry than my stomach. Oh, how I wish I could help!

I open my mouth to say something, then close it back. What is there to say? Poor Charlie needs a home, but I don't. I so wish Wheezy had asked for him instead.

7

———————

Is there any way I could help Charlie, I wonder, but before I can figure out anything, Ella brings Wheezy back. He's still wheezing, but he's got this big smile on his face like somebody promised him hotdogs for dinner.

"How you doing, boy? Look at you! Don't you look handsome? Wanna go for a walk?"

I'm always up for a walk, so I wag my tail politely and wait while Ella hands him a lead and he clips it to my collar.

"Let's go," he says, and we follow Ella to the door. I glance back to see Charlie, his curly ears so low you can't even see them, following us with sorrowful eyes. But he's a champ, and he wags his tail as we leave.

"Good luck, Ranger. Have a great life! You deserve it!"

The bitter smell of his sadness reaches me as the door slams shut behind us, but there's so much going on out here that I forget. The icy air smells of dead leaves and mud. I can swear I sniff a cat not far away. Car engines roar up and down the street, and an ambulance stuck in traffic wails like a cat in heat but isn't going anywhere. The grass feels wet and stiff under my paws, and a sudden gust of wind ruffles my coat. This is the life, I tell myself, inhaling this glorious chaos after the kennel's endless dullness. The wind smells like gasoline and freedom, and something stirs inside me.

How about an escape? My heart picks up the pace as I scan the narrow yard with tired grass along the low concrete building, and the six-foot-tall wire fence topped with razor wire that surrounds it. It's not looking good.

And why not try a home, for once? Charlie sure loves them. He thinks there's nothing better. Even Prozak loved having a human to look after. And Dog knows I saw plenty of dogs walking their humans, and they all looked well-fed and content. The dogs, I mean. Not those Dachshunds, though. Those two looked absolutely ridiculous with their yellow hooded raincoats and those booties, and they knew it. And those poodles, with haircuts so awful that even cats laughed at them. A Yorkipoo had his human push him in a stroller. Can you even call that a walk?

But most dogs looked fat and happy. Their humans served them food and gave them treats. They slept inside when it rained and didn't have to worry about frostbite, poisoned bait, or fighting some stinky rottweiler over a soggy pizza box. They got food every day, and they were never left alone.

But none of them was free.

And none of them seemed to mind.

Wheezy pulls on his leash.

"Good boy, Ranger. Sit."

I sit. He gives me a biscuit.

"Lie down."

I do. Another biscuit makes its way into my tummy.

"Come here."

I come. Another treat is waiting for me.

Wheezy shakes his head and grins from one ear to the other with delight.

"He's awesome," he wheezes, scratching my ears just so. I lean into his hand.

"Right there, a bit more to the left."

He laughs and obliges.

"What a good boy!"

Ella shrugs, unconvinced. She knows better.

"Be careful with cats, though. Ranger doesn't like cats."

"Who does?" Wheezy asks. "Surely not me."

"OK, then. If you're sure... Ranger is already micro-chipped, dewormed, and up to date with his shots. He needs to get neutered, but we wanted to let him recover after his other surgery. He should be good for it next month. Bring him back, and we'll have our vet do it for you."

"OK."

"And don't hesitate to call if you have any trouble."

"I'll call, but we'll have no trouble. I'm used to dogs. And Ranger here is such a good boy."

"OK, then."

Ella sighs and opens the gate. Wheezy takes me back to his car, which is the same. I recognize the smell of cold cigarette smoke and dead dear. He opens the back door and unclips my collar.

"Get in, boy."

I wag my tail and bark.

"Good luck, Charlie. He's all yours!"

I turn tail and fly away like the wind.

8

I ran and ran and ran. After being locked in forever, my paws ate up the asphalt. I ran down sidewalks, across deserted parks, through crowded parking lots. I ran until my paws burned, my tongue hung to my knees, and my chest felt about to explode. I ran until I was sure the humans couldn't catch me.

Only then did I stop to breathe. Where was I?

I had no clue.

But I knew when I was. It was winter.

I'd been too hot under my collar to notice my breath misting the air, the naked trees, and the frosty white grass. But now that I had chilled, I shivered as the blizzard cut through my coat like I was naked and the ice froze my paws. My belly rumbled, reminding me it was past time for my kibble, and, for the first time, I wondered if running away had been a good idea.

If I stayed with Wheezy, I'd be somewhere warm with my belly full of kibble, getting ready to curl up for a nap. But I wasn't. I was somewhere in an empty open field, whipped by a sharp wind that meant business, and with nothing that smelled like food for miles. I'd been so afraid of getting caught that I had rushed past all the fast-food places and the dumpsters where I could find something to eat, and there was nothing like that here.

No shelter either. No sheds, no porches, no trees. Nothing but frozen dirt as far as I could see.

Oh well. It is what it is.

I wished I could head back, but I didn't dare. What if they're still looking for me? So I pushed forward.

I walked and walked, sniffing for smoke. Smoke means humans, therefore food. But there was nothing. Nothing but frozen dirt, barren fields, and a foul murder of crows circling above me and laughing.

I kept walking.

The day turned to dusk, and it got even colder. Before long, a moonless night tightened its icy grip around me.

I kept walking.

It started snowing. Fat flakes tumbled down from the sky, covering the harsh frozen dirt with a blanket of softness. I tried a mouthful of snow. It felt good. It softened my parched throat, soothed my paws, and dulled the sharp emptiness in my belly. It wasn't food, but it was all I had, so I ate it until I felt full.

When my paws wouldn't take me any further, I curled with my nose under my tail, and the snow covered me before long. I tried to sleep, but I couldn't. My paws ached, and my stomach grumbled, reminding me I had traded my food, warmth, and shelter for this.

I hoped Charlie was having a good time.

I woke up stiff with cold. I dug myself out of the snow, shook, and looked around. Yesterday's barren fields had turned into a white sea of untouched snow that glittered in the morning sun, and that ugly wind had stopped.

I gulped as much snow as my belly could hold and got going. I didn't know how far my next meal was, but I knew I had to get moving, or else.

I walked and walked. The snow was shoulder-deep, and the field looked like it lasted forever. I kept walking until a bush showed up, then another. Then a tree, then another, and before you could say "Kibble," I was deep in the woods. The snow was thin here. It barely covered the thick bed of needles, and cedar scent filled my nose. Not bad, though I'd have preferred bacon, or a burger. Even kibble. But there was none of that, so I kept walking.

I was trembling with hunger when I noticed something moving in the corner of my eye. Dinner, I thought, and I leaped like a mad dog, but that dratted chipmunk was already halfway up the tree when I got there. He stopped on a crooked branch to laugh at me, and I never hated anyone more. Not even cats. I barked a curse at him and kept going.

By nightfall, I'd chased two more chipmunks and a squirrel. They all escaped and laughed at me. I hoped their escape would hurt them as much as mine did.

I dug a hole to shelter for the night behind a fallen trunk. I no longer felt hungry, but I trembled with cold and shook with exhaustion. I needed food, and soon, or I was doomed, but I no longer had enough strength to return to the shelter. All I could do was go forward.

Curled in my shelter with my nose under my tail, I thought about Charlie. I hoped Wheezy had taken him home, and his new place was everything he hoped for.

As for me, I was free. But I promised myself that if I lived to see another winter, I won't be spending it outside.

9

———————

It's been a harsh winter. Come spring, I'm nothing but fur and bones, but I know the bad times are over. Once the snow melts and the days grow long, there's no more sleeping on an empty belly, limping on frost-bitten paws, or shivering in the snow. I found shelter in a boarded house that keeps out the rain and some of the wind, and I live the good life. In the morning, I soak the sun in the park, looking for the playground kids to drop their cookies. Come noon, I lie in the shade outside McDonald's, enticing humans to drop a fry or two, and wag my tail at the soft-hearted ones who give me the last bite of their burger. If all else fails, I raid the dumpsters at night and fight the stray cats for a cold pizza crust, gnawed-on chicken bones, and spoiled deli cuts.

Being free to go where I want and do what I want is worth going to bed hungry once in a while, and even fighting the unwise strays who encroach on my territory. I seldom fight, but when I do, I win. After surviving the winter, this summer I grew strong and tough. I know every nook and cranny of my kingdom, from the holes in the fence that let me escape the men in the van, to when the best dumpsters get filled. It was touch and go for a while, but it now looks like I made the right choice the day I ditched Wheezy at the shelter.

Until today.

I'm heading to my place after an awful, rotten day. It's been raining since dawn, so there were no kids at the playground this morning. And no cookies. Oh, well, I told myself, there's always McDonalds. Hungry and soaked to the skin, I hustled to their parking lot, but no human would sit outside in that deluge. A long line of cars clogged the drive through, but the morose drivers didn't spare me a glance, let alone a fry or a burger. And, like that wasn't bad enough, I discovered they put a lock on my favorite dumpster, the one behind KFC.

Oh well. It's gonna be better tomorrow, I mumble as I shuffle home in the rain. But I'm not even there and I know something's off. I'm used to sniffing trouble from afar, so my hackles are already up as I crawl through the fence. I haven't yet seen the squatter, but I smell big trouble, like freaking pit-bull sized trouble. Still, I can't give up my home without a fight, even if I know I can't win.

I've never fought a pit bull, but I know they're tough, stubborn, and bred to fight. But I've never seen a monster like this.

My heart races to break out of my chest as I storm in. The intruder jumps to his paws, growling like a chainsaw, then bursts into a threatening, deep-throated bark as he snarls his yellow fangs at me. It's dark in here, but I can still see his brindle chest is twice my size, and the small porcine eyes stuck to the sides of his wide head burn with rage.

"Get lost, you ugly mutt," he snaps, "If you don't want to end up as my dinner."

"Says who?" I bark, fluffing myself to look bigger and resisting the urge to run.

"I do," he growls like he's gargling nails.

"And who, pray tell, are you?"

"I'm the Bloody Fang of Hickory."

"Nice to meet you. Fang. I'm Ranger, and this is my place."

"Was. Now it's mine. Go find yourself another place, or I'll rip you to shreds before you can say bone."

His stiff legs in a fighting stance and his nasty snarl tell me he's not kidding, and I know that a fight won't end well for me. He's twice as big and thrice as nasty, and looks like he was bred to fight.

So what do I do? Fight him when I know I can't win and get myself ripped to shreds? Or turn around and leave with my tail between my legs? Nobody would know it but me, but that's enough.

His stomach growls and I get an idea. I wag my tail politely.

"Hey Fang?"

"What?"

"Did you have dinner?"

He cocks his big, ugly head and stares at me.

"Dinner?"

"Yes. As in, did you eat anything?"

"Not in a while."

I wag my tail in empathy.

"Neither did I, and I'm famished. How about I take you out for dinner?"

His stance softens. The hair on his neck settles down as he starts slobbering, but his red eyes are still suspicious. Time to load it on.

"You look like an outstanding guy, but you must be new in the area, otherwise I'd have heard about you. I live here, so I know the best places. And there's plenty of room here for both of us until you find your own place. I'll even help you, if you want."

He cocks his head left as his muddled thoughts swirl around his thick brain. But I don't let him think for too long.

"How about barbecue? What kind of ribs do you prefer? Short or spare?"

His eyes glimmer with hope.

"Short."

"Me too. They're fattier and juicier, and I love that awesome crunch! I know a place that does them right, just down the road. They should be delivering soon."

He's still thinking, but a pool of slobber has gathered at his feet.

"We should get going, otherwise this Rottweiler..."

"Let's go," he says.

Before we head out, we sniff each other's bottoms, as per protocol, then our muzzles. I crawl out through the fence and he follows, but he's much bigger, so he gets stuck. I wait until he digs himself out, then we head down the main road. I never take this road, because this is where the men in the van like to hang out, looking for suckers. This would be a good time for them to show up, I think, but sadly, they're not here today.

We trot to the Outback's parking lot. Their dumpster has the best food in town, and we get there just as they're getting ready to close. The last cars are leaving just as we reach the dumpster.

"There you go," I say. "You'll thank me later."

The smell of barbecue is so strong it makes me weak at the knees. My stomach gets growling and I drool like crazy, but I know better than to jump in the dumpster at closing time, when they're bringing out the last of the trash.

Fang doesn't. He jumps in and starts gnawing as I crawl under the bushes to watch.

He's still gorging himself when a skinny kid brings over the last bags of trash and throws them in. From inside, Fang barks a deep throated threat. The kid screams and slams the lid shut, locking him in.

Once again, Mom was right. It's better to be smart than good-looking.

10

A great summer, that was! Good weather, food aplenty, and I even got to toy with the men in the van, who started chasing me again. They learned my places and set clever traps baited with hotdogs and meatballs. Once, they almost got me by the tail, but I flashed my fangs and growled at them, and they stepped back. I loved to watch them and stole their bait just for sport.

But then the days grew shorter, and the leaves started turning. Another harsh winter was coming, and that shelter started looking better. You couldn't go places, but at least it was warm and dry, and it came with food and company, though some of those mongrels weren't the kind you'd want to meet in a dark alley. But others were friendly, like Charlie, and sniffing the breeze with them sure beat shivering in the snow.

But I couldn't. My freedom was all I had.

I kept going, even when my paws were raw from the ice, and my belly growled with hunger. Gone were the cookies in the park and the outdoor diners at McDonalds. I sometimes ate nothing but snow before curling up in my nest, telling myself that spring was just around the corner. Still, I struggled on.

I was so weak I was dizzy with hunger the day I saw that squirrel digging in the snow across the road. I was too starved to think. I just took off like a rocket.

The squirrel saw me and laughed. She headed up the tree, but I was almost there, so I leaped.

A terrible screech hurt my ears. Before I could see it, something smashed into me and threw me flying. High in the air, I spun, I twisted and turned to fall back on my paws. I had almost done it when the ground crashed into me, robbing me of my breath. I opened my eyes to see a car's wheels.

I shook my head to clear the fog, then tried to crawl away, but my paws wouldn't listen.

"You OK, pup?"

A wide-eyed kid with red hair stared at me through thick glasses. Great, I thought. Just what I needed: a human. I tried to run, but my legs disagreed.

"I'm so sorry, Bud! Let's get you checked out."

I growled in protest, but he didn't listen. He picked me up, put me in his car, and took me to the vet. Before you could bark "Milk-Bone," I found myself back at the shelter.

"Ranger! It's you! You're back! Just look at you, will you?"

Ella leans over me with her eyebrows knitted together and her hands on her hips, and she doesn't smell happy. She reminds me of Mother when she caught me chasing cars.

I flatten my ears in remorse and look. I see nothing.

"You're just skin and bones, all covered in scratches and bruises. I bet you have fleas, too. You could have had a forever home and your own human to keep you warm and fed, but no. You had to run away."

I tuck my tail and look guilty, hoping she'll cut it out, but no. All the time she cleans my ears and clips my toenails, she keeps mumbling.

"You need to learn that there are more important things in life than roaming the streets and chasing squirrels, Ranger. You can't live your life running in the streets, stealing food and frightening children. You need to settle and behave like a civilized dog. We'll need to find you a family to take care of, and..."

You think I listened? Think again. I like Ella, but she's touching my toes, and all I can think about is hoping she doesn't cut off my toes with that clipper.

When she's finally done talking, she takes me back to the kennel and locks me in Charlie's old crate. I sniff around for him, but he's gone. I hope Wheezy took him home.

Fortunately, the shelter is full of dogs of all breeds and all colors looking to kill time, so it's not hard to make friends, even though we're too far apart to smell each other's butts. Still, we get to sniff the breeze and bark stories.

Two cells over, there's a Great Dane as big as a horse. When he wags his tail and hits the wall sounds like a beaten drum, but he's friendly.

"How ya doing, kid? What's your name?"

"Fair to middling. I'm Ranger. How about you?"

"I'm Thor. I'm a Great Dane," he barks, and the whole shelter shakes.

"No kidding. I wouldn't have guessed. How come you're here?"

"My Hooman said I needed an operation for my bad hip and he can't afford it, so he surrendered me."

"No wonder. I can't imagine how he could afford your food," a rat-faced chihuahua yaps from the cell to my left.

"Shut up, Guacamole, you troublemaker. After biting that kid, you have no room to talk."

"It wasn't my fault. He pulled my tail as I ate."

Thor turns to me.

"That's chihuahuas for you. They blow up at the drop of a poop, and they take no responsibility whatsoever. I've never met one who was ever wrong."

"Just shut up already," growls the black curly mutt across from me. "One can't even catch a beauty nap in this joint."

Guac chortles.

"No nap could ever fix your ugly face, Versace. If you slept for a week, you'd still..."

Versace flicks his tail at Guacamole and turns to me.

"Never mind the rat dog. Those yappy things never grow up. If you don't mind my asking, you look like you live in the streets?"

"I do."

"Wow! That's awesome! And so rare, these days. Humans fear stray dogs. They say we carry diseases and reproduce out of control, but I know better. They want us all corralled under their paw. They don't want us, dogs, to unite..."

Thor yawns.

"There he goes again. Ever since his human dropped him off because he wasn't purebred and hypoallergenic, he's been barking about changing the world."

"The world is in dire need of changing. Just look at it! From wars to climate change, there's nothing but man-made disasters! We, dogs, need to take charge. Just think about what the world would be like if it was run by dogs. We'd sniff each other's butt every morning, and we'd all get along!

Guacamole shakes.

"The world has already changed, and not for the better. I remember when I was only a pup and..."

I don't know what else he has to say, because I fall asleep. I didn't choose to be here, but it is what it is. At least I'm warm, fed, and safe for now. A good night's sleep, and I'll start planning my escape.

11

But what's the big rush? Shelter life isn't bad. We get two meals of crunchy kibble every day; I have a warm bed, and the guys to chit-chat with. It sure beats freezing in the streets, and every day gets us closer to spring.

Because, no matter what Ella says, the street is where I belong. It's my home. I know she means well, but she can't see inside my heart. She's just a human, so she doesn't understand the call of open spaces, the joy of running unleashed, and the exhilaration of howling at the full moon. To me, nothing matters more than my freedom. I wasn't made to be contained. I need to be free more than I need to eat.

That's what I used to think. Then the door opened, and my life changed.

I felt it even before I saw her. Her scent hit my nose, and my heart started racing. Then I glimpse her elegant black muzzle, her warm amber eyes, and that sexy long tail, and I know my life has changed forever.

The boys sniff her too and go nuts.

"Hello, baby. *Sprachen Sie Deutch*?" Guacamole yaps, showing his crooked yellow teeth.

"Look at the sexy tail on that bitch," Thor mutters.

"A German Shepherd? Here in the shelter? Are you for real?" Versace growls.

I want to bark at them to shut up, but I'm speechless. My eyes glued to her backside, I drool all over my blanket like a love-sick puppy, drinking in her scent.

She ignores us, like a proper lady. She sniffs every inch of her cage, as one does, then curls with her lovely nose on her paws and closes her eyes like she's napping. But I know better. She smells sad and anxious, just shy of despondent, and my heart aches for her.

I wait for the boys to go back to cleaning their privates before I bark to introduce myself.

"Hello, beautiful lady. How delightful to meet you. What's your name?"

She cracks open one eye and glances at me down her sexy muzzle. My insides melt.

"I'm Madeline Rose Kahn Van Jones. Maddie to my friends. How about you?"

"I'm Ranger."

"Just Ranger?"

I spare an unkind thought for Prozak, who only gave me one name, then I remember I'd be nameless if it wasn't for him, and feel ashamed. I'm almost as ungrateful as a human.

"Just Ranger. The name-callers were busy that day. And Ranger is more than I need. Most of the time, it's just 'Hey, you,' 'Flea-bag,' or 'Get away from me, you mangy mutt.'"

She shudders from her shiny black nose to the tip of her tail.

"Really? How rude! Who said that?"

I wag my tail.

"Just about everyone I ever meet. You wouldn't believe the kind of folks you bump into when you live in the streets. But enough about me. Let's speak about you. What's a lovely lady like you doing here?"

She fluffs her hackles and tells me. Long story short, it turns out that Maddie was in charge of a human. When he got sick, his daughter took him to a kennel for old humans, then dropped Maddie at the shelter.

"This is terrible! I need to get out!" she growls, and my heart breaks. I just found her. I can't lose her already!

"But why? This isn't that bad. They give us food and water, and it's warm. The streets are freezing. Why not wait until spring?"

Maddie shakes like she's slogged through mud.

"You don't understand. Jones is my human and my responsibility, and I must find him. I promised I'll make sure he dies in his own bed, and I failed."

That sounds a bit morbid, but who am I to judge? I almost died when I got shot in the forest, then again when I froze in the fields. The bed must be more comfortable.

"Even so, what's the hurry? Can't you wait and kill him in spring? It's only a few weeks away, and we'll escape together."

Maddie glares at me and flashes her teeth.

"You don't get it, do you? I must escape now."

I wag my tail to placate her, but she's done with me. She turns around, sets her nose on her paws, and covers it with her tail to tell me I stink.

She'll get over it, I think, when Ella comes in. She goes from cage to cage to inspect us and take our pictures on her little phone.

She stops by my cage.

"Smile, Ranger," she says.

I wag my tail and do my best to look good. She takes two pictures of me, then moves to Guacamole.

"I wonder what that's all about," Guac mumbles.

Versace cocks his head.

"You don't know? Didn't you hear her call the vet the other day?"

"No."

"They're counting heads for the neutering clinic. You boys are about to sing soprano."

12
______

Say what?

My stomach flips, and my hackles go up by themselves. I knew humans are control freaks. They must always know where you are, when, and with whom, but this is going too far.

"Not gonna happen. Not to me," I growl.

Versace cocks his head.

"Really? And how exactly do you plan to stop them?"

That, I don't know. But I know I wouldn't let humans take control of my love life, especially now that I finally found the girl of my dreams. I'd do anything, and I mean anything, to be with her. And just like that, the answer comes to me loud as a sledgehammer and clear as spring water.

"Maddie?"

She doesn't move. She pretends she's asleep, but I can see her left ear twitch.

"Get ready. We're leaving tomorrow night."

She jumps to her paws.

"We are? How?"

Truth be told, I have no idea. Well, I have an idea. I know exactly how I can escape, but as for her? I need to come up with a plan.

"I'll tell you tomorrow."

Maddie's eyes brighten with joy.

"Really?"

"Of course."

Maybe. I hope so. Dog willing.

I lay my nose on my paws and start thinking. That gets my ears itchy. I scratch them, then remember I haven't cleaned my privates since this morning. I clean them really well, and by the end, I'm so tired I need a nap. I don't know if you noticed, but thinking is hard work, and everything else wants to get in the way.

I nap for a while, then start thinking again. My thoughts run through my brain like baby squirrels chasing each other up a tree. It's downright exhausting. If I was out, I'd go for a run to clear my mind, but I'm locked in this darn cage, so all I can do is to pace back and forth. So I do, until I notice my bed.

Now that's something! I set to work. By the morning, I've ripped that bed into a thousand tiny little shreds, and my plan is ready and solid.

Time for another nap. I curl in the middle of my artwork and fall asleep. I wake up with Maddie's eyes burning holes in my brain.

"Well?"

"You're still on?"

"Of course."

"OK then. Tonight's tech is the pimpled kid who's always on his phone. He's too lazy to close the cage doors while he cleans them and brings in the food and the water. Wait until he opens my cell, then yell as if someone's flaying you alive. Roll on the ground and scream, pretending you're dying. As soon as he opens your door, dash out after me. I'll show you the way out."

"What if he cleans my crate first?"

"Then I'll do the squealing. But wait for me; otherwise, you won't get far."

Maddie cocks her head in deep thought. She doesn't know if she should trust me. No wonder. We haven't even sniffed each other's butts. And she's a purebred German Shepherd, which is the most paranoid breed on earth if you leave out the Dobermans and the Rotties. The Malinois are more neurotic, the Dutch Shepherd more athletic, and the Border Collies more hyper. Still, as for paranoia, the German Shepherds are in a class of their own.

I can smell her thoughts from three cells away, and I know exactly when she makes up her mind, since her scent turns from the acrid bitterness of indecision to buttery smooth.

"OK."

I try to catch another nap to prepare for the showdown, but the morning tech wakes me up. She stares at what's left of the bed with her hands on her hips.

"Shame on you, Ranger. What did that bed do to you? You've been here for weeks, and you've never done something like this. And now? Shame on you! BAD DOG!"

The whole kennel, dozens and dozens of dogs, all go silent. None of them did anything, but they heard the 'B' word, and they're mortified. They all stink of guilt, from Thor, who'd slept throughout the process, to Guacamole, who nobody suspected of having anything resembling a conscience.

All but me. I don't feel guilty one bit. In a free dog's world, that word doesn't exist.

But this is not about me. It's about that pulverized bed, and its consequences. I don't mind getting punished, but I don't need any changes in our daily routine that could affect my escape plan.

One thing Mother taught me before her unfortunate collision with that truck was to always stay calm in an argument. Whoever loses control loses the fight, she said. When your opponent turns bitter, act sweeter than a Krispy Kreme doughnut. If they growl, wag your tail. When they bark, listen. But when they bite... But that's not important right now. Nobody bit anyone yet.

I sit and wag my tail politely.

"I sincerely regret your failure to see the necessity of my efforts. I didn't undertake this work lightly. I would have been more than happy to run around, or maybe chew on a marrow bone to help me focus, but my present living circumstances denied me these options. Unfortunately, I had to satisfy myself with whatever tools I had available to perform my planning."

Thor's jaw hits the floor. Guac's head tilts so low I worry it came out of joint. Maddie's round eyes look at me in wonder.

The tech shakes her head and goes to get a broom.

Advantage me.

13

———

The Escape

This day feels like it drags forever. Tonight, I either escape with the love of my life and my family jewels, or I lose not only her trust, but an essential part of who I am. Sure, I can run the streets and raid dumpsters just as well without my balls, but those things matter to me, especially now that I found love.

To pass the time, I clean them really well, then I curl to catch a nap. I wake up and clean them again. When I start cleaning them for the third time, Guacamole growls at me to stop.

"Stop that, for Dog's sake, or you'll wash them away."

"He's worried he won't see them tomorrow," Versace says.

"It's really no big deal," Thor growls. "The vet puts you to sleep and you don't feel a thing. You're a little sore when you wake up, and you have to wear one of those darn cones for like a week, but after that, you won't even remember to miss them. I don't."

"Sure he will," Guacamole yaps, pointing his long nose at Maddie, who's curled in the back corner of her cage, pretending she's asleep.

"No, I won't," I bark. "Maddie and I will blow this joint tonight. You guys take care. In a day or two, I'll leave a pee-mail by the fence to tell you how it went."

Versace looks at me with new respect.

"Good for you, Ranger. You sure have balls, my friend! I wish I could go with you."

"No, you don't," Guacamole snorts. "A diva like you wouldn't last one day in the street. And who would you bark your speeches to, about the subjugation of dogs by the humans? Here, we don't have a choice, but nobody would listen to your diatribes if they're free to run away. You're much better off right here."

"Like you have room to talk, you yappy rat," Versace growls, glaring at him down his elegant black nose like he stinks.

They keep at it, but I curl with my nose under my tail to catch another nap, since I need all the strength I can gather. I wake up just as the pimply kid comes to clean our cages.

"Are you ready?" I ask Maddie.

"Yep."

"Atta girl," I bark, and stick out my nose out to watch the kid's progress.

He leaves the hallway door open, as usual, as he cleans our cells. He's got his earbuds in his ears and bobs his head up and down as he mops the first cage. When he's done, he moves to the second, sloshing the mop and paying no attention whatsoever to the dog inside it, just like I expected. I wag my tail at Maddie to tell her that everything is going just as planned, but her ears are flat, and her tail tucked in. She smells worried.

The kid moves to her cell and opens the door. It's now or never.

I drop to the ground and start squealing like I'm getting flayed while also getting my toe nails clipped and my best bone stolen, but the kid doesn't hear a thing. He keeps mopping and nodding. He's almost done cleaning Maddie's cell, and my heart freezes. Once he's done with her cage and locks the door, it's all over.

By now, my friends and every other dog in the kennel are barking and squealing and howling. They jump on the grates to rattle the doors, but the kid keeps mopping. Like really? Are you deaf, dude?

That's when Maddie springs into action. She gets into his face, flashing her police-quality fangs, barks up a storm, then grabs the business end of his mop.

The kid startles. He jumps back, his earbuds fall out, and he finally hears the ruckus. He turns to see what's going on in the kennel, while I shriek and roll on the floor like I'm dying.

"What the heck?"

He rushes to my crate and opens the door. I jump to my paws and blast out that cage like a bullet from a rifle, knocking him down in the process. I dash down the hallway to the door. Maddie follows, and, before you can say "hot dog", we're out of the kennel.

"Good job, everyone! This way, baby," I bark.

We sprint down the narrow hallway, then hook a left to the small storage room where they keep the straw bales they use for our bedding. A wintery breeze smelling like gasoline and freedom comes in through the small open window under the ceiling.

"That's the window they always leave open for ventilation. Can you get to it?" I ask Maddie.

Her ears go flat. She looks doubtful, and for good reason. The window is Dog-awful high. She has to jump almost six feet to grab onto it, but she's a fighter and gives it her all. She takes a deep breath and claws her way to the topmost bale, then leaps to grab the window frame.

Not even close.

Somewhere behind, the kid's screaming for help.

Maddie steps back to take a running start. She plants her paws, leaps on the highest bale, then claws her way up the concrete wall. Two more inches and...

She falls back.

The ruckus behind us reached new heights. Dogs bark, a

phone rings, the kid shouts, and heavy steps pummel the hallway. They're getting close.

Maddie turns to me. Her ears are down and her lovely amber eyes so sad they break my heart.

"Sorry, Ranger, I can't do it. I'm too old. You go."

"Are you kidding? I'm not going anywhere without you. Let's do this."

I stand under the window to give her a paw up. I plant my back paws and stretch my front paws up the wall as high as I can, making my body into a ladder.

"Go, baby. Run!"

Maddie dashes from the door, climbs the straw bales, and plants her paws on my back. She grabs the windowsill and claws her way up. Before you can say "Beggin' Strips," she's out the window. Thank Dog.

I'd love to follow her, but I first want to give her time to run. I block the door, snarling, slobbering, and barking like I'm rabid. The kid runs back and slams the door behind him when he sees me.

That's the ticket! I step back to get a running start, and I'm out the window faster than a hotdog through the hatch. I fly and twist through the air, then land on my head. Darn. For the first time in my life, I wish I was a cat.

I sniff for Maddie's trail to follow her, but she's right here, next to me, and my heart swells with joy.

"You're still here, baby? I tried to hold them back as long as I could to give you time to escape!"

She looks at me with her pretty eyes, then licks my nose, and my insides melt. I lick her back, just as the shelter door opens, and a flashlight spears the darkness.

We take off, shoulder to shoulder, in the greatest night of my life.

"I love you, baby," someone growls, and I figure out it's me.

I'm free, and in love. Life doesn't get better than this!

14

I'm not the kind of dog who brags to anyone who'd listen about how he's got the longest tail and wags it better, so I won't get into details about what Maddie and I did after we escaped that evening, other than we ran down the frozen streets until our followers lost us. I knew the men with the van would look for us soon, but for now, we're together. And since we, dogs, live in the present, we'll let the future take care of itself.

Sniffing Maddie's butt for the first time was like magic. Her nose tasted like kibble and honey, and my insides melted whenever she licked my nose.

We ran shoulder to shoulder, chasing our shadows under the silver moon until our chests burned and our tongues touched our knees. Our paws froze, but our hearts burned with love.

I took Maddie to my place and showed her how to squeeze in through the hole in the fence, and, just like that, we were home. We curled around each other to keep warm through the night; We went chasing squirrels in the morning, and in the evening I taught her how to dump dive. I taught her which bags were worth ripping apart and which ones weren't. Like those from the vegans, and from the darn composters who wouldn't throw away a banana peel, let alone a slice of bacon.

I'd never been so in love, and I knew I would never be again. To me, Maddie's scent was better than dead fish, and her growls sweeter than kibble getting poured into my bowl. Every wag of her tail sent my heart into a tailspin, and her every snort felt precious. Our days were magical, and our nights enchanted, but they were shorter than a bulldog's nose.

Before long, Maddie started missing her human. I knew she thought about him, because I could smell the scent of her guilt from the other side of the garbage bin. That's how I knew she'd be leaving me before she did.

Sure enough, we curled together one evening, and she looked at me with her sad puppy eyes. She licked my nose, then flattened her ears and growled.

"I'm so sorry, Ranger. I hate to do this, but I have to go. I love you with all my heart, but Jones is my responsibility. He's old and lonely, and he has no one but me. I must take care of him."

"How about other humans?" I asked. "You said he had a daughter."

"Gwen? She doesn't care a bit about him. She's just there for the taking. She threw away all his beloved books, and she even got rid of me, so I could do nothing to help him. No, there's nobody to help him other than me. I have to go."

My heart broke. But I could not give up without a fight.

"How about your freedom, my love? Isn't it wonderful to do whatever you want whenever you want it? Don't you like chasing squirrels and rummaging the dumpsters for tasty finds? Don't you love eating snow and rolling in the mud? Aren't you happy here?"

"I do, of course, I do. And even more than all that, I love you. But Jones is my responsibility, and I will never be happy if I don't fulfill my mission. Being with you is fun, and it gives me tremendous joy. But happiness is something else. I cannot be happy unless I do the right thing."

I shook my head to rearrange my thoughts, but they didn't fall into place. I cocked my head left, then right, then left again, but I still couldn't understand. How could she throw away her freedom for some human? How could she forget all the magic we shared to go live between four walls? How could she love me so little that she'd leave me? I tried again.

"But I love you, Maddie. I love you like I never loved before. Please stay."

She tucked her tail between her legs and flattened her ears until they seemed to vanish.

"I love you too, Ranger. I love you more than I can say. But I must go."

That was that, then. After we said our last goodbyes, I watched her wave her sexy tail for the last time and disappear into the darkness, my heart heavier than a full dumpster. The bone of my heart had chosen a human over me, and I couldn't wrap my mind around that. But there was nothing I could do.

I waited for her to be gone, then followed her like a shadow. Even though she'd abandoned me, I still had to keep her safe. I had to make sure that she didn't fall prey to the men in the van, got hit by a car, or got struck by some other danger. Because, no matter how brilliant and strong my Maddie is, she didn't grow up in the street, so she doesn't know its risks like I do. I must protect her.

She ran through the frozen empty streets without even glancing back until she reached a tiny house between four maples, in a street I knew well. How on earth did I never see her there? I must have been busy chasing squirrels.

She sniffed the mailbox, as one does, and left a pee-mail to tell me she made it, then went to look inside. Heartbeats later, her hackles went up all the way, and she burst in through the doggie door, growling like a lawnmower and barking up a storm. Something was happening, and she had to intervene. My hackles went up. I got ready to follow her and help, but my terrible aversion to the humans' houses kept me back. But for Maddie, I'd do anything, so I stepped forward to follow when a human female wearing someone else's fur blasted out through the door. She jumped in the car in the driveway and drove away.

Atta girl, Maddie! Nicely done! That was fast.

I got closer and peeked in through the window. My Maddie sat with her lovely head in an old man's lap. He petted her ears, whispering softly, and she closed her eyes.

I wondered if she was thinking about me.

15

Those first days without Maddie were the worst of my life. Wherever I went, whatever I did, all I could see was that she wasn't there. Without her, my old place was empty. Rummaging in the garbage bins alone was no fun, and the frozen streets were even colder. Even pizza crust didn't taste like pizza without her; as for chasing squirrels? I almost gave it up.

How could I feel so lonely and forsaken in the exact same place I had lived my whole life alone? I'd been here for years, and Maddie was with me for just a few days, but when she left, she took with her all my joy. Without her, nothing was the same.

When my loneliness hurt me more than my hunger, I'd sneak to her house and sniff her mailbox. Once in a while, she left me a message to tell me she was okay. I did too, but I lied. My life was empty without her. Still empty or not, it went on.

But then something happened. When that awful winter was over and spring came, I got worried. Maddie's pee-mails smelled off.

I couldn't put my toe on what was wrong, but I sniffed something different. Maddie's scent had changed, and I worried she was sick.

I waited by her mailbox every night, hoping to see her, but she never came out at night. I got so worried I even went there in daylight, risking meeting the men with the van, and I waited there until my tail froze, but she still didn't come.

My stomach growled. I needed to eat. The nights had shrunk, and the snow had turned into mud, but the parks were still empty, and few people sat to eat outside McDonalds, so I'd gotten thin as a rake. I glanced at the sun. Halfway down. Too early for the dumpster, I thought, so I shuffled to my favorite gas station. You never know when some kind soul throws you the last bite of their doughnut or even a meatball from their sub.

Not today. I waited and waited, but there was nothing. Cars came and went, spewing clouds of stinky fumes. Harried humans ran inside and out, warming their hands around cups of coffee, but there was no sign of food anywhere. Maybe it's late enough for the dumpsters, I thought, when the skinny kid at the counter stuck his head through the door.

"Hey!"

I jumped to my paws.

"Catch."

Something flew my way, and I caught it as it twisted through the air. It was a hot dog, which was ironic since I was half frozen.

I wagged my tail in thanks and was about to inhale it, but something stopped me. An irrepressible urge overtook me, and my paws broke into a run by themselves, taking me back to Maddie's house.

I stop by the mailbox and look in. Nothing seems changed, and still, something's different. I don't know why, but I have to see Maddie, no matter what. I tuck my tail between my legs, flatten my ears, and drag my sorry self to the door.

I have never, ever entered a human house, other than the kennel. And the vet. But those weren't proper houses, and I didn't go in there by choice. And now, here I stand, on her doorstep.

I sniff the door. She's home. So is her human. But there's something else, something I never sniffed, but it smells oddly familiar.

I drop the hot dog and bark.

"Maddie?"

"Ranger? Is that you?" she answers from inside.

"May I see you?"

Things happen inside. Maddie barks, something squeaks, someone shuffles, then the door screeches open.

"Come in, Ranger."

16

———

Before stepping inside, I check the human at the door like I'm looking to buy him. He's an old male smelling like barbecue, smoke, and Maddie. His sweater has a hole, his glasses are dirty, and he doesn't smell unkind.

But entering this house I don't know is the hardest thing I've ever done. What if they lock me in?

I'd better run while I can.

But Maddie is inside.

I wish she'd come to the door.

But she doesn't.

My heart frozen with fear, I pick up the hotdog I dropped on the doorstep. I flatten my ears, tuck my tail between my legs until it touches my chin, and drag myself in.

The door slams shut.

I'm trapped. My heart flips. I'm about to fly through the window.

"Ranger?" Maddie barks from the other room.

I force myself to put one paw in front of the other. It feels like forever until I finally see her. Her amber eyes are warm and loving, and she looks as beautiful as ever. My heart melts. I drop the hotdog under her nose.

"I got this for you."

Her loving tongue licks my nose, and all is well with the world.

I lick her back.

"How are you, Maddie?"

She wags her tail.

"Real busy. But happy."

She lays her dark muzzle over a row of orange blobs that hang from her belly like grapes. There's six of them, and they all smell like me. I sniff them one by one, wondering how something so beautiful can exist as my heart bursts with joy. I wag my tail and lick Maddie's nose.

"I'm so proud of you, baby. These pups are the most beautiful sight I've ever seen. Other than you, of course."

"Thank you, Ranger."

She starts licking them, one after the other, from their noses to their toes. I sit and watch, but there's six of them and it's slow going. I don't know what to do.

I guess that's it.

I wag my tail left to say goodbye, and turn towards the door. Maddie's human wipes his foggy glasses on his half-eaten sweater.

"Ranger, would you like to join us for dinner?" he asks.

I cock my head in surprise. Really? He has only two legs and no tail. As for his teeth... Just forget it. He really doesn't look like he's any good at dumpster diving.

And then there's the kids...

I glance at Maddie. She wags her tail yes.

"Great idea, Jones. What's for dinner?"

"Meatloaf with mashed potatoes and gravy. And vanilla ice cream."

Maddie's amber eyes look at me over the squirmy pups who are elbowing each other to raid the milk bar.

"Stay, please?" she growls.

Oh boy. My tail tucks between my legs to touch my skin as I look for an escape.

The doggie door is open, thank Dog.

"Anything for you, my dear."

17

I stayed for dinner. I came back for breakfast. Then dinner again.

Being with Maddie and watching the kids grow filled my heart with pride and joy. The pups got bigger, brighter, and cuter every day. They were a hoot, unless they got confused and looked for the milk bar on my belly.

Maddie's human wasn't that bad, either. Jones, she called him. He sat around all day, watching the pups, reading in his chair, or watching a black box with moving shadows that smelled like nothing. Then he made dinner, and I helped with the dishes. We got along just fine, other than when it rained. He pursed his lips and didn't smell happy when I came in after my cleansing mud bath. But I allowed him to wipe my feet, and he seemed to settle.

But one day he sniffed and glared at me above his glasses.

"Sorry, Ranger, but if you're going to be here with us, I'm afraid we'll have to set some ground rules. There'll be no rolling in dead fish before coming inside. I'm afraid you need a bath. And a flea treatment."

I glanced at Maddie.

"What's he saying?"

She sighed.

"Sorry, Ranger. Humans can't even smell their own feet, but they have this curious adversity about dead fish. Don't get me wrong, I think you smell fantastic, but..."

"But I did it for you! I went out of my way to go to the pier."

"And I appreciate it. But..."

Jones clipped his leash to my collar and grabbed a bottle smelling of mint.

"Let's go give you a bath."

I looked at Maddie.

"What's that?"

She flattened her ears.

"That's the medicated shampoo. That's what he'll wash you with."

My hackles went up.

"Oh, no, he won't. Are you kidding? No way," I growled. "I'll take my own mud bath when I feel like it, thank you very much. Don't come near me with that."

"Common, Ranger. Being clean isn't bad," Maddie said. "You may even like it."

"No."

Jones tried to drag me out. I flashed my teeth and growled.

"I said no."

Jones stared at me above his glasses.

"Really?"

"Really."

Jones looked at Maddie.

"Sorry, Maddie, but I can't have that in the house. If your friend is to stay with us, he'll have to abide by the rules. I said nothing about the mud, about chewing the table leg, or about stealing the butter. I couldn't even find the wrapping paper. But I can't have the house smell like dead fish."

Maddie turned her pleading eyes to me.

"Common, Ranger. A nice bath won't be that bad. It's gonna even help with the itching."

"What itching?"

"You may not notice, but you scratch like crazy. Even when you sleep."

"No, I don't."

"Yes, you do. You have fleas. And it's bad enough if you give them to me, but I don't want you giving them to the kids."

"Everyone has fleas. They are a part of life."

"Not everyone. I never had fleas before I met you. When I came back from your place, I had three baths before I got rid of them. You think I liked it?"

I stared at her, dumbfounded. The love of my life was a bitch. How could that be?

"But Maddie, I can't let that stand. I have to draw a line somewhere, otherwise who knows what he'll do next? He'll want me to wipe my feet before coming inside and maybe even not roll in the mud. I can't do that.

"Why not? I can."

"But Maddie, I already gave up so much! I stopped barking at squirrels when I'm inside, and I gave up dumpster diving since last week. I never even roam at night! I wake up when he does and go to bed at night. I can't give up the dead fish! I can't lose that last bit of my freedom!"

"I'm sorry, Ranger."

The puppies squeaked, and she forgot about me. She got busy soothing and feeding them.

My heart heavy, I headed to the door. I stopped and glanced back.

"Bye, Maddie."

"Bye, Ranger."

She was so busy with the kids she didn't spare me a glance.

18

And just like that, I found myself alone again, just because I wouldn't let Jones bathe me with that filthy shampoo. The love of my love had betrayed me for a human. It was hard to believe, but it was true.

I went to my old home, the parks, and the dumpsters. It was the same life I'd always had, the only life I ever wanted, but it felt empty. I missed Maddie, and I missed the kids. And believe it or not, I even missed Jones.

The old coot wasn't so bad when you got to know him better. He scratched my ears better than I could, and cooked better than the dumpster, though not as well as McDonald's. And he doted on Maddie and the kids. I think he even had a soft spot for me; otherwise, why get me that huge marrow bone when I ate the table leg? I'd never even seen one like that. I almost wished I hadn't left it with Maddie, but it was mostly spent when I left.

Oh well. Life is what it is.

Between working the parks, raiding the dumpsters, and avoiding the men in the van, that summer passed like a dream. Then the days grew shorter again. The leaves turned, and the wind started smelling of snow. Another winter was on its way, and if I said I looked forward to it, I'd be lying like a human.

I still checked Maddie's mailbox every other day to make sure she and Jones were OK. I'd watched the pups go to forever homes, one by one. Strangely, I was glad they didn't end up in the street, like me. Freedom is wonderful, but loneliness is terrible. And an empty heart hurts more than an empty belly.

I was heading to Maddie's mailbox when the first snowflake melted on my nose. I licked it off and sniffed the mailbox. Nothing new. I glanced at the house. The windows were dark, and the place was quiet, but there was something...

I inched closer.

Something smelled fishy, and it wasn't me.

I circled the house, sniffing every inch, but couldn't put my paw on what was wrong. I had to go inside.

Fortunately, I knew all the escape routes I had learned long ago. The doggie door in the mudroom opened both ways, and I could reach the garage door opener with my paw if I stretched. If all else failed, I could jump through the dining-room window.

I'd often planned on escaping that place, but I'd never imagined breaking in. But there I was. I squeezed in through the doggie door, and the air burned my nose. Something was terribly wrong.

I ran to the living room, then the kitchen. Nothing.

I rushed to Jones' bedroom. The door was closed.

"Maddie? Are you there?" I barked.

Nothing.

My heart flipped. Whatever this was, it wasn't good.

I jumped on the door, trying to open it, but my paws couldn't work that darn knob! I tried with my teeth, but no luck.

My heart got racing, and my hackles went up. I needed to hurry.

I stepped back to get a running start and threw myself headfirst through the frosted glass door. The glass broke into a thousand pieces, with a crash louder than a gunshot. Shards of glass cut my face and my shoulders, and I tasted salty blood on my nose, but I had no time for that. Despite the ruckus, Maddie lied there in her bed, and Jones snored under his blankets like I hadn't made enough noise to wake the dead.

"Maddie?" I barked.

She didn't budge.

I grabbed her by the scruff of her neck and pulled her out through the hole in the door, and she still didn't wake up. I hoped she didn't get cut, but I had no time to check. I jumped on the wall to push the button and opened the garage door, then I dragged Maddie out into the yard.

I left her there and went back for Jones, but no matter how I tried, I couldn't drag him out. I couldn't find the scruff of his neck, and his pajamas ripped apart when I pulled.

I stopped to think. I wasn't getting anywhere. Jones was too heavy to drag and too big to pull through the door. I had to do something else.

I left him there and ran back out to Maddie and tried everything I could think to wake her up: I licked her nose; I barked in her ears; I even bit her toes. She kept snoring.

The time had come to make the choice of my life, but it was easy. Between Maddie's life and mine, I chose hers.

I barked and barked, then went and scratched at the neighbor's doors until every light went on in the street. When the humans came out to see what happened, I took them to Maddie, then inside to Jones.

The police came, then the ambulance, lights flashing and sirens wailing like cats in heat. They took Jones on a stretcher, then some human put Maddie in his car and drove her away. I tried to follow the car, but I wasn't fast enough. I stopped to breathe, and a net closed around me.

The men with the van had nabbed me at last.

19

Ella shook her head when she saw me.

"You, Ranger? Back again, are you? I've never met an escape artist like you. They should have called you Houdini. But it sounds like you outdid yourself this time."

She gave me a bath that smelled like Jones's shampoo. Phew! I forsook my happiness to escape that, and now I get it anyhow? I tried to run, but she had me tied but good. There was nothing I could do but put up with that indignity. She cleaned and dressed my wounds, then took me to a cell.

My old friends were all gone. What happened to them? I wondered. Did Guacamole lose his balls? Did Thor find a human willing to take him, bad hip and all? Did Versace start a revolution? Probably not, since the world hadn't changed for the better. Dogs were still caged, and humans still ran the world, with their rules, their opposable thumbs, and their stinky shampoos.

The new dogs in the shelter stared at me like I had three ears.

"Are you the hero?" growled a scruffy terrier

"The what?"

"Someone said they were bringing in some hero who saved a human. Is that you?"

I didn't know what a hero was, nor did I care. I lay my nose on my paws and fell asleep.

Days and nights passed, and nothing happened. I slept a lot and ate a little. I burned to know what had happened to Maddie and Jones, but no one would tell me, so I started to plan my escape. I'll go back to the house and find out, I told myself, but this time it was tricky. The window I'd escaped through was barred, and the shelter door was always closed, even when the pimply kid was on duty. My escape chances looked dismal.

One day, Ella clipped a leash to my collar.

"Where am I going?"

She didn't answer, and a horrible thought crossed my mind. Last time I was here, I'd ran off just in time to escape the spay day. Was it coming?

My heart froze. I looked right and left for a way to escape, but Ella knew all my tricks. I was doomed. My hackles went up as I braced myself for the vet.

But it wasn't the vet. It was Jones.

My heart skipped a beat.

"Maddie?"

"Hi, Ranger. How are you doing?"

"Fine, thanks. Where's Maddie?"

"I… I came to thank you for saving my life. I knew I should have had that chimney cleaned, but between this and that, I forgot. That's what got us in trouble. They said that both Maddie and I got poisoned with carbon monoxide. The doctor told me I'd be dead if I breathed that poison for another hour. I'm only alive because of you. So, I came to thank you."

"Sure, whatever. Maddie?"

"And invite you to dinner. I made spaghetti and meatballs. And apple pie."

I stared at him in despair. How thick can humans be?

"Maddie?" I barked.

"Maddie…"

"Maddie?"

"She said to tell you there'll be hot dogs too."

For more Amazing Dog Stories, read **Charlie, The Scaredy Cat.**

ABOUT THE AUTHOR

Rada Jones was born in Transylvania, next door to Dracula's Castle. Growing up between communists and vampires taught her that humans are fickle, but one can always depend on dogs and books. That's why she read every book, including the phone book – too many characters, too little action – and took home every stray, from dogs to frogs.

After immigrating to the US to join her husband, she went to med school and worked in the ER for years, but she still speaks like Dracula's cousin.

When the night shifts got old, she left the ER to write. Her **ER CRIMES** series feature serial killers, some of them lovely people, and Dr. Emma Steele, an ER doc with a moody daughter and a love for wine. If you're into dark humor, check out her medical essays in **STAY AWAY FROM MY ER**. But if you're into dogs, the **K-9 HEROES** series is right for you.

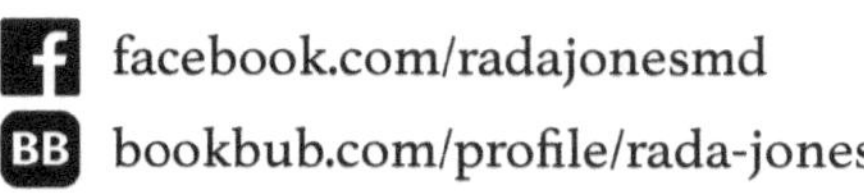

BOOKS BY RADA JONES

BECOMING K-9: A Bomb Dog's Memoir

BIONIC BUTTER: A Three-Pawed K-9 Hero

K-9 VIPER: The Veteran's Story

LOVELY K-9: A Prison Puppy

K-9 RAMBO: The Dutch Master

K-9 PROZAK: POW

K-9 HEROES: Final Mission

K-9 HEROES (BOOKS 1,2,3)

MORE K-9 HEROES (BOOKS 4,5,6)

MOM: A Dog Story Prequel to BECOMING K-9

RANGER: The Escape Artist

CHARLIE:: The Scaredy Cat

OVERDOSE: An ER Psychological Thriller

MERCY: An ER Thriller

POISON: An ER Thriller

DO HARM: A Cruise Thriller

SEE EVIL: A Cruise Thriller

TAKE LIVES: A Cruise Thriller

ER CRIMES: The Steele Files

Box Set: Books 1-3

<u>STAY AWAY FROM MY ER</u>, and Other Fun Bits of Wisdom

<u>DRIVING ITALY</u>: A Cheeky Travel Memoir

<u>EXPLORING KENYA</u>: A Cheeky Safari Memoir